PUFFIN BOOKS

EDITOR: KAYE WEBB

LITTLE OLD MRS PEPPERPOT

These gay, amusing stories are quite unlike any others you
may know. Most of them are about Mrs Pepperpot – a salty
old character with good sharp wits which never deserted her,
even when she shrank to about a thousandth part of her
original size. She just woke one morning to find herself the size
of her own kitchen pepperpot – and how she was ever to get out
of bed was a problem! She had a husband to think of too, the
house to clean, and a week's wash in soak – not to mention the
cat and dog to whom she must now look painfully like a bird
or mouse. However, she was not one to take fright, or to give
in easily; and what she could not manage herself, she con-
trived to make others do for her. There her sharp wits came in.
She did not remain pepperpot size for ever after that morning, but could never be certain, day or night, when it would
happen again. She had no warning of it. All in a moment she
found herself pepperpot size, and some time later – snap! –
she was herself again.

A delightfully good-humoured imagination invented these
adventures and escapes, and laughter bubbles through them
constantly. They are intended primarily for the delight of
young listeners, from three, four, or five (depending on the
reading habits of the home), but they will also entertain the
parents and grandparents who read them aloud.

Also available: *Mrs Pepperpot to the Rescue*, *Mrs Pepperpot
in the Magic Wood* and *Mrs Pepperpot's Outing*.

ALF PRØYSEN

Little Old Mrs Pepperpot

AND OTHER STORIES

TRANSLATED BY MARIANNE HELWEG

ILLUSTRATED BY BJÖRN BERG

PUFFIN BOOKS

Puffin Books, Penguin Books Ltd, Harmondsworth, Middlesex, England
Penguin Books, 625 Madison Avenue, New York, New York 10022, U.S.A.
Penguin Books Australia Ltd, Ringwood, Victoria, Australia
Penguin Books Canada Ltd, 2801 John Street, Markham, Ontario, Canada L3R 1B4
Penguin Books (N.Z.) Ltd, 182–190 Wairau Road, Auckland 10, New Zealand

—

The stories in this volume have been selected
from two books, *Little Old Mrs Pepperpot* and
Mrs Pepperpot Again, first published in England
by Hutchinson 1959 and 1960
This selection published in Puffin Books 1961
Reprinted 1963, 1965, 1966, 1967, 1969, 1970, 1971, 1972 (twice),
1973, 1974 (twice), 1975, 1976, 1977 (twice), 1978, 1979, 1980

—

This selection copyright © Penguin Books, 1961
All rights reserved

—

Made and printed in Great Britain
by Richard Clay (The Chaucer Press) Ltd,
Bungay, Suffolk
Set in Monotype Baskerville

Contents

Little Old Mrs Pepperpot

THERE was once an old woman who went to bed at night as old women usually do, and in the morning she woke up as old women usually do. But on this particular morning she found herself shrunk to the size of a pepperpot, and old women don't usually do that. The odd thing was, her name really was Mrs Pepperpot.

'Well, as I'm now the size of a pepperpot, I shall have to make the best of it,' she said to herself, for she had no one else to talk to; her husband was out in the fields and all her children were grown up and gone away.

Now she happened to have a great deal to do that day. First of all she had to clean the house, then there was all the washing which was lying in soak and waiting to be done, and lastly she had to make pancakes for supper.

'I must get out of bed somehow,' she thought, and, taking hold of a corner of the eiderdown, she started rolling herself up in it. She rolled and rolled until the eiderdown was like a huge sausage, which

fell softly on the floor. Mrs Pepperpot crawled out and she hadn't hurt herself a bit.

The first job was to clean the house, but that was quite easy; she just sat down in front of a mouse-hole and squeaked till the mouse came out.

'Clean the house from top to bottom,' she said, 'or I'll tell the cat about you.' So the mouse cleaned the house from top to bottom.

Mrs Pepperpot called the cat: 'Puss! Puss! Lick out all the plates and dishes or I'll tell the dog about you.' And the cat licked all the plates and dishes clean.

Then the old woman called the dog. 'Listen, dog; you make the bed and open the window and I'll give you a bone as a reward.' So the dog did as

8

he was told, and when he had finished he sat down on the front door-step and waved his tail so hard he made the step shine like a mirror.

'You'll have to get the bone yourself,' said Mrs Pepperpot, 'I haven't time to wait on people.' She pointed to the window-sill where a large bone lay.

After this she wanted to start her washing. She had put it to soak in the brook, but the brook was almost dry. So she sat down and started muttering in a discontented sort of way:

'I have lived a long time, but in all my born days I never saw the brook so dry. If we don't have a shower soon, I expect everyone will die of thirst.' Over and over again she said it, all the time looking up at the sky.

At last the raincloud in the sky got so angry that it decided to drown the old woman altogether. But she crawled under a monk's-hood flower, where she stayed snug and warm while the rain poured down and rinsed her clothes clean in the brook.

Now the old woman started muttering again: 'I have lived a long time, but in all my born days I have never known such a feeble South Wind as we have had lately. I'm sure if the South Wind started blowing this minute it couldn't lift me off the ground, even though I am no bigger than a pepperpot.'

The South Wind heard this and instantly came tearing along, but Mrs Pepperpot hid in an empty badger set, and from there she watched the South Wind blow all the clothes right up on to her clothes-line.

Again she started muttering: 'I have lived a

long time, but in all my born days I have never seen the sun give so little heat in the middle of the summer. It seems to have lost all its power, that's a fact.'

When the sun heard this it turned scarlet with rage and sent down fiery rays to give the old woman sun-stroke. But by this time she was safely back in her house, and was sailing about the sink in a saucer. Meanwhile the furious sun dried all the clothes on the line.

'Now for cooking the supper,' said Mrs Pepperpot; 'my husband will be back in an hour and, by hook or by crook, thirty pancakes must be ready on the table.'

She had mixed the dough for the pancakes in a bowl the day before. Now she sat down beside the bowl and said: 'I have always been fond of you, bowl, and I've told all the neighbours that there's not a bowl like you anywhere. I am sure, if you really wanted to, you could walk straight over to the cooking-stove and turn it on.'

And the bowl went straight over to the stove and turned it on.

Then Mrs Pepperpot said: 'I'll never forget the day I bought my frying-pan. There were lots of

13

pans in the shop, but I said: "If I can't have that pan hanging right over the shop assistant's head, I won't buy any pan at all. For that is the best pan in the whole world, and I'm sure if I were ever in trouble that pan could jump on to the stove by itself." '

And there and then the frying-pan jumped on to the stove. And when it was hot enough, the bowl tilted itself to let the dough run on to the pan.

Then the old woman said: 'I once read a fairy-tale about a pancake which could roll along the road. It was the stupidest story that ever I read. But I'm sure the pancake on the pan could easily turn a somersault in the air if it really wanted to.'

At this the pancake took a great leap from sheer pride and turned a somersault as Mrs Pepper-pot had said. Not only one pancake, but *all* the pancakes did this, and the bowl went on tilting and the pan went on frying until, before the hour was up, there were thirty pancakes on the dish.

Then Mr Pepperpot came home. And, just as he opened the door, Mrs Pepperpot turned back to her usual size. So they sat down and ate their supper.

And the old woman said nothing about having been as small as a pepperpot, because old women don't usually talk about such things.

Mrs Pepperpot
and the mechanical doll

IT was two days before Christmas. Mrs Pepper-pot hummed and sang as she trotted round her kitchen, she was so pleased to be finished with all her Christmas preparations. The pig had been killed, the sausages made, and now all she had to do was to brew herself a cup of coffee and sit down for a little rest.

'How lovely that Christmas is here,' she said, 'then everybody's happy – especially the children – that's the best of all; to see them happy and well.'

The old woman was almost like a child herself because of this knack she had of suddenly shrinking to the size of a pepperpot.

She was thinking about all this while she was making her coffee, and she had just poured it into the cup when there was a knock at the door.

'Come in,' she said, and in came a little girl who was oh! so pale and thin.

'Poor child! Wherever do you live – I'm sure I've never seen you before,' said Mrs Pepperpot.

'I'm Hannah. I live in the little cottage at the edge of the forest,' said the child, 'and I'm just going round to all the houses to ask if anybody has any old Christmas decorations left over from last year – glitter or paper-chains or glass balls or anything, you know. Have *you* got anything you don't need?'

'I expect so, Hannah,' answered Mrs Pepper-pot, and went up into the attic to fetch the card-board box with all the decorations. She gave it to the little girl.

'How lovely! Can I really have all that?'

'You can,' said Mrs Pepperpot, 'and you shall have something else as well. Tomorrow I will bring you a big doll.'

'I don't believe that,' said Hannah.

'Why not?'

'You haven't *got* a doll.'

'That's simple; I'll buy one,' said Mrs Pepper-pot. 'I'll bring it over tomorrow afternoon, but I must be home by six o'clock because it's Christmas Eve.'

'How wonderful if you can come tomorrow afternoon – I shall be all alone. Father and Mother both go out to work, you see, and they don't get back until the church bells have rung.'

So the little girl went home, and Mrs Pepper-pot went down to the toy-shop and bought a big doll. But when she woke up next morning there she was, once more, no bigger than a pepper-pot.

'How provoking!' she said to herself. 'On this

19

day of all days, when I have to take the doll to Hannah. Never mind! I expect I'll manage.'

After she had dressed she tried to pick up the doll, but it was much too heavy for her to lift.

'I'll have to go without it,' she thought, and opened the door to set off.

But oh dear! it had been snowing hard all night, and the little old woman soon sank deep in the snowdrifts. The cat was sitting in front of the house; when she saw something moving in the snow she thought it was a mouse and jumped on it.

'Hi, stop!' shouted Mrs Pepperpot. 'Keep your claws to yourself! Can't you see it's just me shrunk again?'

'I beg your pardon,' said the cat, and started walking away.

'Wait a minute,' said Mrs Pepperpot, 'to make up for your mistake you can give me a ride down to the main road.' The cat was quite willing, so she lay down and let the little old woman climb on her back. When they got to the main road the cat stopped. 'Can you hear anything?' asked Mrs Pepperpot.

'Yes, I think it's the snow-plough,' said the cat,

'so we'll have to get out of the way, or we'll be buried in snow.'

'I don't want to get out of the way,' said Mrs Pepperpot, and she sat down in the middle of the road and waited till the snow-plough was right in front of her; then she jumped up and landed smack on the front tip of the plough.

There she sat, clinging on for dear life and en-joying herself hugely. 'Look at me, the little old woman, driving the snow-plough!' she laughed.

When the snow-plough had almost reached the door of Hannah's little cottage, she climbed on to the edge nearest the side of the road and, before you could say Jack Robinson, she had landed safely on the great mound of snow thrown up by the plough. From there she could walk right across Hannah's hedge and

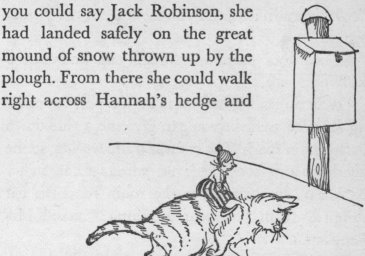

slide down the other side. She was shaking the snow off her clothes on the doorstep when Hannah came out and picked her up.

'Are you one of those mechanical dolls that you wind up?' asked Hannah.

'No,' said Mrs Pepperpot, 'I am a woman who can wind myself up, thank you very much. Help me brush off all the snow and then let's go inside.'

'Are you perhaps the old woman who shrinks to the size of a pepperpot?'

'Of course I am, silly.'

'Where's the doll you were going to bring me?' asked Hannah when they got inside.

'I've got it at home. You'll have to go back with me and fetch it. It's too heavy for me.'

'Shouldn't you have something to eat, now that you've come to see me? Would you like a biscuit?' And the little girl held out a biscuit in the shape of a ring.

'Thank you very much,' said Mrs Pepperpot and popped her head through the biscuit ring.

Oh, how the little girl laughed! 'I quite forgot you were so small,' she said; 'let me break it into little pieces so that you can eat it.' Then she fetched a thimble and filled it with fruit juice. 'Have a drink,' she said.

'Thank you,' said Mrs Pepperpot.

After that they played a lot of good games; ride-a-cock-horse with Mrs Pepperpot sitting on Hannah's knee, and hide-and-seek. But the little girl had an awful time trying to find Mrs Pepperpot – she hid in such awkward places. When they had finished playing Hannah put on her coat and with Mrs Pepperpot in her pocket she went off to fetch her beautiful big doll.

'Oh, thank you!' she exclaimed when she saw it. 'But do you know,' she added, 'I would really rather have *you* to play with all the time.'

'You can come and see me again if you like,' said Mrs Pepperpot, 'I am often as small as a pepperpot, and then it's nice to have a little help around the house. And, of course, we can play games as well.'

So now the little girl often spends her time with Mrs Pepperpot. She looks ever so much better, and they often talk about the day Mrs Pepperpot arrived on the snow-plough, and about the doll she gave Hannah.

Mr Pepperpot buys macaroni

'IT'S a very long time since we've had macaroni for supper,' said Mr Pepperpot one day.

'Then you shall have it today, my love,' said his wife. 'But I shall have to go to the grocer for some. So first of all you'll have to find me.'

'Find you?' said Mr Pepperpot. 'What sort of nonsense is that?' But when he looked round for her he couldn't see her anywhere. 'Don't be silly, wife,' he said; 'if you're hiding in the cupboard you must come out this minute. We're too big to play hide-and-seek.'

'*I'm* not too big, I'm just the right size for "hunt-the-pepperpot",' laughed Mrs Pepperpot. 'Find me if you can!'

'I'm not going to charge round my own bed-room looking for my wife,' he said crossly.

'Now, now! I'll help you; I'll tell you when you're warm. Just now you're very cold.' For Mr Pepperpot was peering out of the window, thinking she might have jumped out. As he searched round the room she called out 'Warm!',

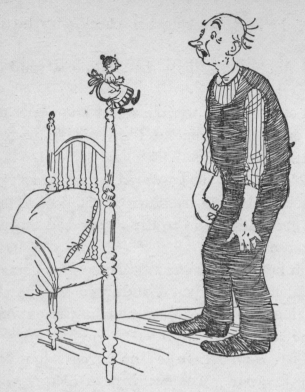

'Colder!' 'Getting hotter!' until he was quite
dizzy.

At last she shouted, 'You'll burn the top of your
bald head if you don't look up!' And there she
was, sitting on the bedpost, swinging her legs and
laughing at him.

Her husband pulled a very long face when he
saw her. 'This is a bad business – a very bad busi-

ness,' he said, stroking her cheek with his little finger.

'I don't think it's a bad business,' said Mrs Pepperpot.

'I shall have a terrible time. The whole town will laugh when they see I have a wife the size of a pepperpot.'

'Who cares?' she answered. 'That doesn't matter a bit. Now put me down on the floor so that I can get ready to go to the grocer and buy your macaroni.'

But her husband wouldn't hear of her going; he would go to the grocer himself.

'That'll be a lot of use!' she said. 'When you get home you'll have forgotten to buy the macaroni. I'm sure even if I wrote "macaroni" right across your forehead you'd bring back cinnamon and salt herrings instead.'

'But how are you going to walk all that way with those tiny legs?'

'Put me in your coat pocket; then I won't need to walk.'

There was no help for it, so Mr Pepperpot put his wife in his pocket and set off for the shop.

Soon she started talking: 'My goodness me,

what a lot of strange things you have in your pocket – screws and nails, tobacco and matches – there's even a fish-hook! You'll have to take that out at once; I might get it caught in my skirt.'

'Don't talk so loud,' said her husband as he took out the fish-hook. 'We're going into the shop now.'

It was an old-fashioned village store where they sold everything from prunes to coffee cups. The grocer was particularly proud of the coffee cups and held one up for Mr Pepperpot to see. This made his wife curious and she popped her head out of his pocket.

'You stay where you are!' whispered Mr Pepperpot.

'I beg your pardon, did you say anything?' asked the grocer.

'No, no, I was just humming a little tune,' said Mr Pepperpot. 'Tra-la-la!'

'What colour are the cups?' whispered his wife. And her husband sang:

> ' *The cups are blue*
> *With gold edge too,*
> *But they cost too much*
> *So that won't do!*'

After that Mrs Pepperpot kept quiet – but not for long. When her husband pulled out his tobacco tin she couldn't resist hanging on to the lid. Neither her husband nor anyone else in the shop noticed her slipping on to the counter and hiding behind a flour-bag. From there she darted silently across to the scales, crawled under them, past a pair of kippers wrapped in newspaper, and found herself next to the coffee cups.

'Aren't they pretty!' she whispered, and took a step backwards to get a better view. Whoops! She

fell right into the macaroni drawer which had been left open. She hastily covered herself up with macaroni, but the grocer heard the scratching noise and quickly banged the drawer shut. You see, it did sometimes happen that mice got in the drawers, and that's not the sort of thing you want people to know about, so the grocer pretended nothing had happened and went on serving.

There was Mrs Pepperpot all in the dark; she could hear the grocer serving her husband now. 'That's good,' she thought. 'When he orders macaroni I'll get my chance to slip into the bag with it.'

But it was just as she had feared; her husband forgot what he had come to buy. Mrs Pepperpot shouted at the top of her voice, 'MACARONI!', but it was impossible to get him to hear.

'A quarter of a pound of coffee, please,' said her husband.

'Anything else?' asked the grocer.

'MACARONI!' shouted Mrs Pepperpot.

'Two pounds of sugar,' said her husband.

'Anything more?'

'MACARONI!' shouted Mrs Pepperpot.

But at last her husband remembered the macaroni of his own accord. The grocer hurriedly filled a bag. He thought he felt something move, but he didn't say a word.

'That's all, thank you,' said Mr Pepperpot. When he got outside the door he was just about to make sure his wife was still in his pocket when a van drew up and offered to give him a lift all the way home. Once there he took off his knapsack with all the shopping in it and put his hand in his pocket to lift out his wife.

The pocket was empty.

Now he was really frightened. First he thought she was teasing him, but when he had called three times and still no wife appeared, he put on his hat again and hurried back to the shop.

The grocer saw him coming. 'He's probably going to complain about the mouse in the macaroni,' he thought.

'Have you forgotten anything, Mr Pepperpot?' he asked, and smiled as pleasantly as he could.

Mr Pepperpot was looking all round. 'Yes,' he said.

'I would be very grateful, Mr Pepperpot, if you would keep it to yourself about the mouse being in the macaroni. I'll let you have these fine blue coffee cups if you'll say no more about it.'

'Mouse?' Mr Pepperpot looked puzzled.

'Shh!' said the grocer, and hurriedly started wrapping up the cups.

Then Mr Pepperpot realized that the grocer had mistaken his wife for a mouse. So he took the cups and rushed home as fast as he could. By the time he got there he was in a sweat of fear that his wife might have been squeezed to death in the macaroni bag.

'Oh, my dear wife,' he muttered to himself. 'My poor darling wife. I'll never again be ashamed of you being the size of a pepperpot – as long as you're still alive!'

When he opened the door she was standing by the cooking-stove, dishing up the macaroni – as large as life; in fact, as large as you or I.

The mice and the Christmas tree

Now you shall hear the story about a family of mice who lived behind the larder wall.

*   *   *

Every Christmas Eve, Mother Mouse and the children swept and dusted their whole house with their tails, and for a Christmas tree Father Mouse decorated an old boot with spider's web instead of tinsel. For Christmas presents, the children were each given a little nut, and Mother Mouse held up a piece of bacon fat for them all to sniff.

After that, they danced round and round the boot, and sang and played games till they were

tired out. Then Father Mouse would say: 'That's all for tonight! Time to go to bed!'

That is how it had been every Christmas and that is how it was to be this year. The little mice held each other by the tail and danced round the boot, while Granny Mouse enjoyed the fun from her rocking-chair, which wasn't a rocking-chair at all, but a small turnip.

But when Father Mouse said, 'That's all for tonight! Time to go to bed!' all the children dropped each other's tails and shouted: 'No! No!'

'What's that?' said Father Mouse. 'When I say it's time for bed, it's time for bed!'

'We don't want to go!' cried the children, and hid behind Granny's turnip rocking-chair.

'What's all this nonsense?' said Mother Mouse. 'Christmas is over now, so off you go, the lot of you!'

'No, no!' wailed the children, and climbed on to Granny's knee. She hugged them all lovingly.

'Why don't you want to go to bed, my little sugar lumps?'

'Because we want to go upstairs to the big drawing-room and dance round a proper Christmas tree,' said the eldest Mouse child. 'You see,

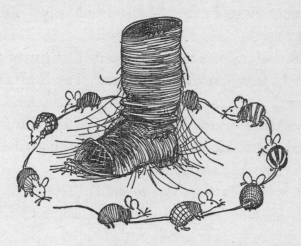

I've been peeping through a crack in the wall and I saw a huge Christmas tree with lots and lots of lights on it.'

'We want to see the Christmas tree and all the lights too!' shouted the other children.

'Oh, but the drawing-room can be a very dangerous place for mice,' said Granny.

'Not when all the people have gone to bed,' objected the eldest Mouse child.

'Oh, do let's go!' they all pleaded.

Mother and Father Mouse didn't know what to say, but they couldn't very well disappoint the children on Christmas Eve.

'Perhaps we could take them up there just for a minute or two,' suggested Mother Mouse.

'Very well,' said Father, 'but follow me closely.'

So they set off. They tiptoed past three tins of herring, two large jars of honey, and a barrel of cider.

'We have to go very carefully here,' whispered Father Mouse, 'not to knock over any bottles. Are you all right, Granny?'

'Of course I'm all right,' said Granny, 'you just

carry on. I haven't been up in the drawing-room since I was a little Mouse girl; it'll be fun to see it all again.'

'Mind the trap!' said the eldest Mouse child. 'It's behind that sack of potatoes.'

'I know that,' said Granny; 'it's been there since I was a child. I'm not afraid of that!' And she took a flying leap right over the trap and scuttled after the others up the wall.

'What a lovely tree!' cried all the children when they peeped out of the hole by the drawing-room fireplace. 'But where are the lights? You said there'd be lots and lots of lights, didn't you? Didn't you?' The children shouted, crowding round the eldest one, who was quite sure there had been lights the day before.

They stood looking for a little while. Then suddenly a whole lot of coloured lights lit up the tree! Do you know what had happened? By accident, Granny had touched the electric switch by the fireplace.

'Oh, how lovely!' they all exclaimed, and Father and Mother and Granny thought it was very nice too. They walked right round the tree, looking at the decorations, the little paper baskets,

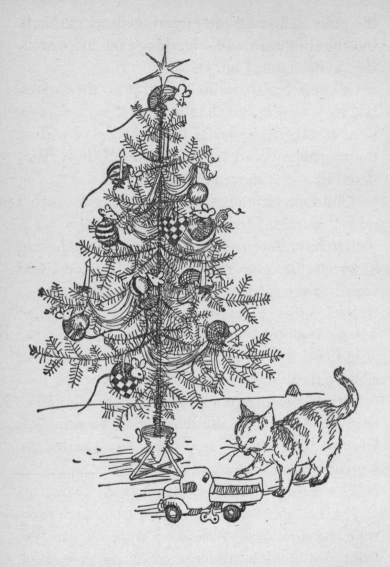

the glass balls, and the glittering tinsel garlands. But the children found something even more exciting: a mechanical lorry!

Of course, they couldn't wind it up themselves, but its young master had wound it up before he went to bed, to be ready for him to play with in the morning. So when the Mouse children clambered into it, it started off right away.

'Children, children! You mustn't make such a noise!' warned Mother Mouse.

But the children didn't listen; they were having a wonderful time going round and round and round in the lorry.

'As long as the cat doesn't come!' said Father Mouse anxiously.

He had hardly spoken before the cat walked silently through the open door.

Father, Mother, and Granny Mouse all made a dash for the hole in the skirting but the children were trapped in the lorry, which just went on going round and round and round. They had never been so scared in all their Mouse lives.

The cat crouched under the tree, and every time the lorry passed she tried to tap it with her front paw. But it was going too fast and she missed.

Then the lorry started slowing down. 'I think we'd better make a jump for it and try to get up in the tree,' said the eldest Mouse. So when the lorry stopped they all gave a big jump and landed on the branches of the tree.

One hid in a paper basket, another behind a bulb (which nearly burned him), a third swung on a glass ball, and the fourth rolled himself up in some cotton wool. But where was the eldest Mouse? Oh yes, he had climbed right to the top and was balancing next to the star and shouting at the cat:

'*Silly, silly cat,*
You can't catch us!
You're much too fat,
Silly, silly cat!'

But the cat pretended not to hear or see the little mice. She sharpened her claws on the lorry. 'I'm not interested in catching mice tonight,' she said as if to herself, 'I've been waiting for a chance to play with this lorry all day.'

'Pooh! That's just a story!' said the eldest who was also the bravest. 'You'd catch us quick enough if we came down.'

'No, I wouldn't. Not on Christmas Eve!' said the cat. And she kept her word. When they did all come timidly down, she never moved, but just said: 'Hurry back to your hole, children. Christmas Eve is the one night when I'm kind to little mice. But woe betide you if I catch you tomorrow morning!'

The little mice pelted through that hole and never stopped running till they got to their home behind the larder wall. There were Father and Mother and Granny Mouse waiting in fear and trembling to know what had happened to them.

When Mother Mouse had heard their story she said, 'You must promise me, children, never to go up to the drawing-room again.'

'We promise! We promise!' they all shouted together. Then she made them say after her *The Mouse Law*, which they'd all been taught when they were tiny:

> *'We promise always to obey*
> *Our parents dear in every way,*
> *To wipe our feet upon the mat*
> *And never, never cheek the cat.*

Remember too the awful danger
Of taking money from a stranger;
We will not go off on our own
Or give our mother cause to moan.

Odd bits of cheese and bacon-scraps
Are almost certain to be traps,
So we must look for bigger things
Like loaves and cakes and doughnut-rings;

And if these rules we still obey
We'll live to run another day.'

Queen of the Crows

DID you know that the woman who was as small as a pepperpot was queen of all the crows in the forest?

No, of course you didn't, because it was a secret between Mrs Pepperpot and me until now. But now I'm going to tell you how it happened.

Outside the old woman's house there was a wooden fence and on it used to sit a large crow.

'I can't understand why that crow has to sit there staring in at the kitchen window all the time,' said Mr Pepperpot.

'I can't imagine,' said Mrs Pepperpot. 'Shoo! Get along with you!'

But the crow didn't move from the fence.

Then one day Mrs Pepperpot had her shrinking turn again (I can't remember now what she was supposed to be doing that day, but she was very busy), and by the time she had clambered over the doorstep she was quite out of breath.

'Oh dear, it's certainly hard to be so small,' she puffed.

Suddenly there was a sound of flapping wings and the crow swooped down, picked up Mrs Pepperpot by her skirt and flew up over the highest fir trees in the forest with her.

'What's the idea, may I ask? You wait till I'm back to my proper size and I'll beat you with my birch rod and chase you off for good!'

'Caw-caw! You're small enough now, at any rate,' said the crow; 'I've waited a long time for this. I saw you turn small once before, you see, so I thought it might happen again. And here we are, but only just in time. Today is the Crows' Festival and *I'm* to be Queen of the Crows!'

'If you're to be Queen of the Crows, you surely don't need to take an old woman like me along?'

'That's just where you're wrong,' said the crow, and flapped her wings; the old woman was heavier than she had expected. 'Wait till we get back to my nest, then you'll see why.'

'There's not much else I *can* do,' thought poor Mrs Pepperpot as she dangled from the crow's claws.

'Here we are; home!' said the crow, and dropped Mrs Pepperpot into the nest. 'Lucky it's empty.'

'It certainly is; I fell right on a spiky twig and grazed my shinbone.'

'Poor little thing!' said the crow. 'But look, I've made you a lovely bed of feathers and down. You'll find the down very snug and warm, and the feathers are just the thing when night falls and the wind begins to blow.'

'What do I want with feathers and down?'

'I want you to lie down and go to sleep,' said the crow. 'But first you must lend me your clothes. So please take off your head-scarf now, and your blouse and your skirt.

'The scarf I want you to tie round my neck, the skirt goes on one wing and the blouse on the other. Then I shall fly to the clearing in the forest where all the crows are meeting for the Festival. The finest-looking crow will be chosen queen, and that's going to be me! When I win I'll think of you. Caw-caw!'

'Well, if you think you'll be any better looking in my old clothes, you're welcome,' said Mrs Pepperpot as she dressed up the crow.

'Hurry, hurry!' said the crow. 'There's another crow living over there in that fir tree on the hill. She'll be dropping in here on her way; we were going to the Festival together. But now that I'm all dressed up I'd rather go alone. Caw-caw-caw!' And off she flew.

Mrs Pepperpot sat shivering in her petticoat, but then she thought of burrowing deep under the feathers and down as the crow had told her to do, and she found she was soon warm and cosy.

Suddenly the whole branch started swaying, and on the end perched a huge crow.

'Mary Crow, are you at home?' croaked the crow, sidling up and poking her big beak over the edge of the nest.

'Mary Crow has gone to the Festival,' said Mrs Pepperpot.

'Then who are you, who are you?' asked the crow.

'I'm just an old woman shivering with cold, because Mary Crow has borrowed my clothes.'

'Caw-caw! Oh blow! She'll be the finest-looking crow at the Festival,' shrieked the crow as she threw herself into the air from the branch. 'But I'll have the scarf off her!'

Mrs Pepperpot lay down to sleep again. Suddenly she rolled right over into the corner of the nest, the branch was shaking so much.

'That'll be another crow,' she thought, and quite right, it was; the biggest crow she had ever seen was swinging on the tip of the branch.

'Mary Crow, Mary Crow, have you seen Betty Crow?'

'I've seen both Mary Crow *and* Betty Crow,' said Mrs Pepperpot.

'Who are you, who are you?' squawked the crow.

'I'm just an old woman shivering with cold because Mary Crow has borrowed my clothes.'

'Caw-caw! What a bore! Now Mary Crow will be the best-looking crow.'

'I'm not so sure about that,' said the old woman, 'because Betty Crow flew after Mary Crow and was going to have the scarf off her.'

'I'll take the skirt, I'll take the skirt!' croaked the biggest crow, and took off from the branch with such a bound that Mrs Pepperpot had to hold on tight not to get thrown out of the nest.

In the clearing in the forest there were lots and lots of crows. They sat round in a circle and, one by one, they hopped into the middle to show themselves. Some of the crows could hop on one leg without touching the ground with their wings.

Others had different kinds of tricks, and the crows sitting round had to choose the best one to be their queen.

At last there were only three crows left. They sat well away from each other, polishing their feathers

and looking very fierce indeed. One had a scarf, the second had a skirt, and the third had a blouse. So you can guess which crows *they* were. One of them was to be chosen queen.

'The crow with the scarf round her neck is the best,' said some of the crows, 'she looks most like a human being.'

'No, no; the crow with the skirt looks best!'

'Not at all! The crow with the blouse looks most dignified, and a queen should be dignified.'

Suddenly something fell with a bump to the ground; the jay had arrived right in the middle of the Festival with a strange-looking bird in its beak.

'Caw-caw! The jay has no business to be here!' croaked all the crows.

'I won't stay a minute,' said the jay. 'I've just brought you your queen!' and he flew off.

All the crows stared at the strange little raggedy bird in the middle of the ring. They could see it was covered in crow's feathers and down, but raggedy crows could not be allowed at the Festival.

'It's against the law!' said the biggest crow.

'Let's peck it, let's peck it!' said Mary Crow.

'Yes, let's hack it to pieces!' said Betty Crow.

'Yes, yes!' croaked all the crows. 'We can't have raggedy birds here!'

'Wait a minute!' said the raggedy bird, and climbed on to a tree-stump. 'I'll sing you a song.' And before they could stop it, it started singing 'Who Killed Cock Robin?' And it knew all the verses. The crows were delighted; they clapped and flapped their wings till the raggedy bird lost nearly all its feathers.

'D'you know any more? D'you know any more?' they croaked.

'I can dance the polka,' said the raggedy bird, and danced round the circle till they were all out of breath.

'You shall be our Queen!' they all shouted. 'Four Court Crows will carry you wherever you wish to go.'

'How wonderful!' laughed the Queen of the Crows. 'Then they must carry me to the house over there by the edge of the forest.'

'What would Your Majesty like to wear?'

'I would like to wear a skirt, a blouse, and a head-scarf,' said the Queen.

Much later that night there was a knock at the cottage door. Mr Pepperpot opened it, and there stood his wife.

'You're very late, wife,' he said. 'Where have you been?'

'I've been to a Festival,' she answered.

'But why are you covered in feathers?'

'You just go to bed and don't trouble yourself,'

said Mrs Pepperpot. She went over and stuck a
feather in the corner of the window.

'Why do you do that?' asked her husband.

'For no reason at all.'

But she really did it because she had been chosen
Queen of the Crows.

Mrs Pepperpot at the bazaar

ONE day Mrs Pepperpot was alone in her kitchen. At least, she was not *quite* alone, because Hannah, the little girl who had had the doll for Christmas, was there as well. She was busy scraping out a bowl and licking the spoon, for the old woman had been making gingerbread shapes.

There was a knock at the door. Mrs Pepperpot said, 'Come in.' And in walked three very smart ladies.

'Good afternoon,' said the smart ladies. 'We are collecting prizes for the lottery at the school bazaar this evening. Do you think you have some little thing we could have? The money from the bazaar is for the boys' brass band – they need new instruments.'

'Oh, I'd like to help with that,' said Mrs Pepperpot, for she dearly loved brass bands. 'Would a plate of gingerbread be any use?'

'Of course,' said the smart ladies, but they laughed behind her back. 'We could take it with us now if you have it ready,' they said. But Mrs

Pepperpot wanted to go to the bazaar herself, so she said she would bring the gingerbread.

So the three smart ladies went away and Mrs Pepperpot was very proud and pleased that she was going to a bazaar.

Hannah was still scraping away at the bowl and licking the sweet mixture from the spoon.

'May I come with you?' she asked.

'Certainly, if your father and mother will let you.'

'I'm sure they will,' said the child, 'because Father has to work at the factory and Mother is at her sewing all day.'

'Be here at six o'clock then,' said Mrs Pepperpot, and started making another batch of gingerbread shapes.

But when Hannah came back at six the old woman was not there. All the doors were open, so she went from room to room, calling her. When she got back to the kitchen she heard an odd noise coming from the table. The mixing bowl was upside down, so she lifted it carefully. And there underneath sat her friend who was now again as small as a pepperpot.

'Isn't this a nuisance?' said Mrs Pepperpot. 'I

was just cleaning out the bowl after putting the gingerbread in the oven when I suddenly started shrinking. Then the bowl turned over on me. Quick! Get the cakes out of the oven before they burn!'

But it was too late; the gingerbread was burnt to a cinder.

Mrs Pepperpot sat down and cried, she was so disappointed. But she soon gave that up and started thinking instead. Suddenly she laughed out loud and said:

'Hannah! Put me under the tap and give me a good wash. We're going to the bazaar, you and I!'

'But you can't go to the bazaar like that!' said Hannah.

'Oh yes, I can,' said Mrs Pepperpot, 'as long as you do what I say.'

Hannah promised, but Mrs Pepperpot gave her some very queer orders. First she was to fetch a silk ribbon and tie it round the old woman so that it looked like a skirt. Then she was to fetch some tinsel from the Christmas decorations. This she had to wind round and round to make a silver bodice. And lastly she had to make a bonnet of gold foil.

'Now you must wrap me carefully in cellophane and put me in a cardboard box,' said Mrs Pepper-pot.

'Why?' asked Hannah.

'When I've promised them a prize for the bazaar they must have it,' said Mrs Pepperpot, 'so I'm giving them myself. Just put me down on one of the tables and say you've brought a mechanical doll. Tell them you keep the key in your pocket and then pretend to wind me up so that people can see how clever I am.'

Hannah did as she was told, and when she got to the bazaar and put the wonderful doll on the table, many people clapped their hands and crowded round to see.

'What a pretty doll!' they said. 'And what a lovely dress!'

'Look at her gold bonnet!'

Mrs Pepperpot lay absolutely still in her cardboard box, but when she heard how everybody praised her, she winked at Hannah with one eye, and Hannah knew what she wanted. She lifted Mrs Pepperpot very carefully out of the box and pretended to wind her up at the back with a key.

Everyone was watching her. But when Mrs Pepperpot began walking across the table, picking her way through the prizes, there was great excitement.

'Look, the doll can walk!'

And when Mrs Pepperpot began to dance they started shouting and yelling with delight, 'The doll is dancing!'

The three smart ladies who had been to see Mrs Pepperpot earlier in the day sat in special seats and looked very grand. One of them had given six expensive coffee cups, the second an elegant table mat, and the third a beautiful iced layer cake.

Mrs Pepperpot decided to go over and speak to them, for she was afraid they had recognized her and thought it queer that she hadn't brought the gingerbread.

The three smart ladies were very pleased when the doll came walking across the table to them.

'Come to me!' said the one who had given the coffee cups, and stretched her hand out towards Mrs Pepperpot, who walked on to it obediently.

'Let me hold her a little,' said the lady with the elegant table mat, and Mrs Pepperpot went over to her hand.

'Now it's my turn,' said the lady with the iced cake.

'I'm sure they know it's me,' thought Mrs Pepperpot, 'that's why they stare at me so hard and hold me on their hands.'

But then the lady with the cake said, 'Well, I must say, this is a much better prize than the gingerbread that the odd old woman offered us today.'

Now she should never have said that; Mrs Pepperpot leaped straight out of her hand and landed PLOP! right in the middle of the beautiful iced layer cake. Then she got up and waded right through it. The cake lady screamed, but people were shouting with laughter by now.

'Take that doll away!' shrieked the second lady, but *squish*, *squash!* went Mrs Pepperpot's sticky feet, right across her lovely table mat.

'Get that dreadful doll away!' cried the third lady. But it was too late; Mrs Pepperpot was on the tray with the expensive coffee cups, and began to dance a jig. Cups and saucers flew about and broke in little pieces.

What a-to-do! The conductor of the brass band had quite a job to quieten them all down. He announced that the winning numbers of the lottery would be given out.

'First prize will be the wonderful mechanical doll,' he said.

When Hannah heard that she was very frightened. What would happen if somebody won Mrs Pepperpot, so that she couldn't go home to her husband? She tugged at Mrs Pepperpot's skirt and whispered, 'Shall I put you in my pocket and creep away?'

'No,' said Mrs Pepperpot.

'But think how awful it would be if someone won you and took you home.'

'What must be must be!' said Mrs Pepperpot.

The conductor called out the winning number, '311!' Everyone looked at their tickets, but no one had number 311.

'That's a good thing!' sighed Hannah with relief. There would have to be another draw. But just then she remembered she had a ticket in her hand; it was number 311!

'Wait!' she cried, and showed her ticket. The conductor looked at it and saw it was the right one.

So Hannah was allowed to take Mrs Pepperpot home.

Next day the old woman was her proper size

again and Hannah only a little girl, and Mrs Pepperpot said, 'You're my little girl, aren't you?'

'Yes,' said Hannah, 'and you're my very own Mrs Pepperpot, because I won you at the bazaar yesterday.'

And that was the end of Mrs Pepperpot's adventures for a long time.

Never take no for an answer

An old woman was hard at work spinning yarn one day when a young mouse came out of the hole by the stove.

'Well, well, fancy seeing you,' said the old woman.

'Peep, peep!' said the little mouse. 'My ma sent me to ask what the yarn is for that you're spinning?'

'It's for a jersey for my husband; the one he has is so worn he can't use it any more,' answered the old woman.

'Peep, peep! I'd better go and tell that to my ma!' And the little mouse disappeared down the hole. The old woman went on spinning, but it wasn't long before she heard a scuffling by the stove and there sat the mouse once more.

'You back again?' she asked.

'Peep, peep! My ma said to ask you who is to have your husband's old jersey when he gets the new one?'

'I'm going to use that myself when I milk the

cows, because my old milking jacket isn't fit to wear any more,' said the old woman.

'Peep, peep! I'd better go and tell that to my ma,' said the mouse, and he was gone. But in no time at all he was back again.

'What d'you want to know this time?' the old woman asked.

'Peep, peep! My ma wants to know who is to have your old milking jacket when you get your husband's old jersey and he gets the new one?'

'The dog is going to have it in his kennel, because his old rug is so thin it's no good any more.'

'Peep, peep! I'd better go and tell that to my ma,' said the little mouse, and darted away to his hole by the stove. But he had hardly popped in before he popped out again.

'That was quick!' said the woman. 'What is it now?'

'Peep, peep! My ma wants to know who is to have the dog's old rug when he gets your old milking jacket and you get your husband's old jersey and he gets the new one?' said the mouse all in one breath.

'You can have it, if you like,' said the old woman.

'Peep, peep! Thank you *very* much,' said the little mouse. 'Now there'll be an eiderdown for *our* bed as well!' And he was so pleased he sang this song:

> *'Oh me, oh my!*
> *We'll soon be as snug*
> *As a bug in a rug,*
> *What do you think of that!*
> *Come and see me any time*
> *I'll make you up another rhyme,*
> *But please don't bring the cat.'*

Mr Learn-a-lot and the singing midges

ONE warm summer night Mrs Midge said to her daughters, 'We'll go and visit Mr Learn-a-lot, the schoolmaster.'

'What do we want to do that for?' asked the young midges. There were three of them: Big Sister Midge, Middle Sister Midge, and Wee Sister Midge.

'We're going to sing to him. You're all so good at singing now, it's a pleasure to listen to you, and Mr Learn-a-lot is such a good judge of music.'

So they all flew off to Mr Learn-a-lot's house and hovered outside his bedroom window. Mrs Midge peered through the glass while her daughters all talked at once in high, squeaky voices:

'Is the window shut, Mama?'

'Won't he open it, Mama?'

'Can't we get in, Mama?'

'I expect he'll open the window when he goes to bed,' said Mrs Midge.

'He's opening the window now, Mama!'

'Can we go in now, Mama?'

'What shall we sing for him, Mama?'

'Not so fast, children, there's no hurry. Let Mr Learn-a-lot get nicely into bed first.'

'He's climbing into bed now, Mama! He's in bed, really he is, Mama! Wouldn't it be dreadful if he fell asleep before he heard our singing, Mama?' squeaked all the little midges. But Mrs Midge was sure the schoolmaster would wake up again when they started singing.

'I think Big Sister Midge had better go in first,' she said.

'All right, but what am I to sing, Mama?'

'You can sing the song about "We midges have not got ...",' said Mrs Midge, and settled herself with her two younger daughters behind the curtain. 'And remember to fly in a circle over his head. If he likes your song he will sit up in bed. Now off you go!'

And Big Sister Midge flew round and round in a circle over Mr Learn-a-lot's head and sang this song:

        'We midges have not got a couple of beans
        Yet in summer we all are as happy as queens,

For every night in a swoon of delight
We dance to the tune of our dizzy flight,
And all we need to keep in the pink
Is a tiny drop of your blood to drink.'

Three times she sang the same verse, and she was beginning to think Mr Learn-a-lot didn't care for her song at all. But suddenly he sat bolt upright in bed.

'Come back! Come back, child!' whispered Mrs Midge.

'Was I all right, Mama?'

'You were very good. Now we'll just wait till Mr Learn-a-lot has fallen asleep again, then it'll be Middle Sister's turn. You can sing the song about "How doth the little busy me" – that is so very funny! There! Now I think it would be all right for you to start. But you mustn't leave off before Mr Learn-a-lot has got right out of bed and is standing in the middle of the floor. Fly a little higher than your sister did. Off you go!'

And Middle Sister Midge sang as loudly as she could while she flew round and round the schoolmaster's head:

> *'How doth the little busy me*
> *Improve each shady hour*
> *By settling on your nose or knee*
> *As if upon a flower.'*

She hadn't sung more than one verse before Mr Learn-a-lot threw off the bedclothes and tumbled out of bed.

'Come back, come back!' whispered Mrs Midge.

'Wasn't I good?' said Middle Sister as she arrived back all out of breath. 'And I wasn't a bit afraid of him!'

'That'll do; we midges are not in the habit of boasting,' said Mrs Midge. 'Now it's Wee Sister's turn.'

'What shall I sing?' asked the smallest midge with the tiniest voice you ever heard.

'You can sing our evening song – you know – the one that goes:

> *'The day is done and all rejoice*
> *To hear again this still small voice.*
> *May the music of my wings*
> *Console you for my little stings.*

'That's just the thing for tonight,' Mrs Midge added thoughtfully.

'Oh yes, I know that one,' said Wee Sister; she was very pleased her mother had chosen one she knew.

'I expect it will be the last song tonight,' said Mrs Midge, 'and don't worry if you don't get right through it. If Mr Learn-a-lot suddenly claps his hands you must be sure to come back to me at once. Will you remember that?'

'Yes, Mama,' said Wee Sister, and off she flew.

Mr Learn-a-lot was lying absolutely still. So

Wee Sister began to sing – all on one top note:

'The day is done –'

Smack! Mr Learn-a-lot clapped his hands together.

'Come back, come back!' called Mrs Midge. But there was no sign of Wee Sister.

'Oh, my darling, sweet wee one, please come back to your mother!' wailed Mrs Midge. No sound – no sound at all for a long time; then suddenly Wee Sister was sitting on the curtain beside them.

'Didn't you hear me calling?' asked Mrs Midge very sternly.

'Oh yes, but you said I was to fly very, very quietly, and that clap of Mr Learn-a-lot's sent me flying right into the darkest corner of the room.'

'Poor darling!' said Mrs Midge. 'But you're safe back now. You've all been very good and very clever girls. And now I'd like to hear what you think of Mr Learn-a-lot?'

Big Sister answered, 'He's nice; he likes the one who sings longest best!'

Middle Sister answered, 'He's very polite; he gets out of bed for the one who sings loudest!'

And Wee Sister said, 'I think he's very musical;

72

he claps the one with the sweetest voice!'

'Yes, yes, that's all very true,' said Mrs Midge; 'but now I will tell you something else about Mr Learn-a-lot. He is not only a very learned gentleman, but he will provide us with the nicest, most enjoyable supper, and we needn't even wake him up. Shall we go?'

'Oh, that is a fine idea!' cried Big Sister, Middle Sister, and Wee Sister Midge, for they always did just what their mother told them.

Poor Mr Learn-a-lot!

Mrs Pepperpot tries to please her husband

THINGS were not very lively at Mrs Pepperpot's house. Mr Pepperpot was in a bad mood – he had been in it for days – and Mrs Pepperpot simply didn't know how to get him out of it. She put flowers on the table and cooked him his favourite dish, fried bacon with macaroni cheese. But it was all no use; Mr Pepperpot just went on moping.

'I don't know what's the matter with him,' sighed Mrs Pepperpot, 'perhaps he's pining for pancakes.' So she made him a big pile of pancakes.

When her husband came in for dinner his face lit up at the sight of them, but as soon as he'd sat down and picked up his knife and fork to start eating, his face fell again; he was as glum as before.

'Ah well!' he said, staring up at the ceiling, 'I suppose it's too much to expect.'

'I've had enough of this!' cried Mrs Pepperpot.

'You tell me what's wrong, or I'll *shrink*, so I will!' (You remember that Mrs Pepperpot had a habit of shrinking to the size of a pepperpot, though not usually, I'm afraid, when she *wanted* to, but at the most inconvenient moments.) 'You have something on your mind, that's quite clear,' she went on. 'But you don't think of me, do you? Watching your face getting longer every day is no joke, I can tell you. Now even pancakes can't cheer you up.'

'Pancakes are all right,' nodded Mr Pepperpot, 'but there's something else missing.'

'What could that be?' asked his wife.

'Couldn't we sometimes have a bit of bilberry jam with the pancakes, instead of just eating them plain?' And Mr Pepperpot gave a great sigh.

At last she understood; it *was* a very long time since she had given him bilberry jam, and that was what the poor man had been missing.

'Well, if that's all you want, I'll go and pick some bilberries this very minute,' said Mrs Pepperpot, and she snatched a bucket from a hook on the wall and rushed out of the door.

She walked rather fast because she was cross with her husband, and as she walked she talked to herself: 'I've got the silliest husband alive,' she muttered. 'I was a fool to marry him. In fact, there's only one bigger fool than me, and that's him. *Oh*, how stupid he is!'

In no time at all she reached the spot in the forest where the bilberries grew. She put her bucket under a bush and started picking into the cup she had in her apron pocket. Every time the cup was full she emptied it into the bucket. Cup after cup went in, until the bucket only needed one more cup to be quite full. But then, just as she had picked the last bilberry into the cup, lo and behold! She shrank to the size of a pepperpot.

'Now we're in a jam, that's certain, and I don't mean bilberry jam!' said the little old woman, who now had a tiny voice like a mouse. 'Still, I expect I can manage to get the cup as far as the bucket if I push and pull hard enough. After that we'll have to think again.'

So she crooked her arm through the handle and dragged the cup along. It was very hard at first, but then she came to an ant-path made of slippery pine-needles; here it was much easier, because the cup could slide along it. And all the time little ants and big ants kept scuttling to and fro beside her. She tried to talk to them.

'How d'you do, ants,' she said. 'Hard at work, I see. Yes, there's always plenty to do and that's a fact.' But the ants were far too busy to answer.

'Couldn't you stop for a minute and talk to me?' she asked. But they just hurried on. 'Well, I shall have to talk to myself; then I won't be disturbing anybody.' And she sat down with her back leaning against the cup.

As she sat there, she suddenly felt something breathe down her neck; she turned round, and saw a fox standing there waving his tail in a friendly sort of way.

'Hullo, Mr Fox. Are you out for a stroll?' said Mrs Pepperpot. 'Lucky you don't know my hens are ... Oh dear! I nearly let my tongue run away with me!'

'Where did you say your hens were, Mrs Pepperpot?' asked the fox in his silkiest voice.

'That would be telling, wouldn't it?' said Mrs Pepperpot. 'But, as you see, I'm rather busy just now; I've got to get this cup of bilberries hauled over to the bucket somehow, so I haven't time to talk to you.'

'I'll carry the cup for you,' said the fox, as polite as could be. 'Then you can talk while we walk.'

'Thanks very much,' said Mrs Pepperpot. 'As I was saying, my hens are … There now! I nearly said it again!'

The fox smiled encouragingly: 'Just go on talking, it doesn't matter what you say to *me*.'

'I'm not usually one to gossip, but somehow it

seems so easy to talk about my hens being ... Goodness, why don't I keep my mouth shut? Anyway, there's the bucket. So, if you would be so kind and set the cup down beside it I'll tell you where my hens are.'

'That's right, you tell me. Your hens will be quite safe with me.'

'They certainly will!' laughed Mrs Pepperpot, 'for they're all away! They were broody, so I lent them to the neighbours to hatch out their eggs.'

Then the fox saw he had been tricked, and he was so ashamed he slunk away into the forest and hid himself.

'Ha, ha, ha! That was a fine trick you played on the fox!' said a voice quite close to Mrs Pepperpot. She looked up and there stood the wolf towering over her.

'Well, if it isn't Mr Wolf!' said Mrs Pepperpot, swallowing hard to keep up her courage. 'The ve ... very person I need. You can help me tip this cup of bilberries into the bucket.'

'Oh no, you can't fool me like you did the fox,' said the wolf.

'I'm not trying to fool you at all,' said Mrs Pepperpot; she had had a good idea and was no

longer afraid. 'You'd better do as I say or I'll send
for One-eye Threadless!'

The wolf laughed. 'I've heard many old wives'
tales but I've never heard that one before!'

'It's not an old wives' tale,' said Mrs Pepperpot

indignantly, 'and I'm not just an old wife; I'm
Mrs Pepperpot who can shrink and grow again all
in a flash. One-eye Threadless is my servant.'

'Ha, ha! I'd like to see that servant of yours!'
laughed the wolf.

'Very well; stick your nose into my apron
pocket here and you'll meet him,' said Mrs
Pepperpot. So the wolf put his nose in her apron
pocket and pricked it very severely on a needle she
kept there.

'Ow, ow!' he shouted and started running towards the forest. But Mrs Pepperpot called him back at once: 'Come here! You haven't done your job yet; empty that cup into that bucket, and don't you dare spill a single berry, or I'll send for One-eye Threadless to prick you again!'

The wolf didn't dare disobey her, but as soon as he had emptied the cup into the bucket he ran like the fox to the forest to hide.

Mrs Pepperpot had a good laugh as she watched him go, but then she heard something rustle near the bucket. This time it was the big brown bear himself.

'Dear me! What an honour!' said Mrs Pepperpot in a shaky voice, and she curtsied so low she nearly disappeared in the bushes. 'Has the fine weather tempted Your Majesty out for a walk?'

'Yes,' growled the big brown bear and went on sniffing at the bucket.

'How very fortunate for me! As Your Majesty can see, I've picked a whole bucket of berries, but it's not very safe for a little old woman like myself to walk in the forest alone. Could I ask Your Majesty to carry the bucket out to the road for me?'

'I don't know about that,' said the bear. 'I like bilberries myself.'

'Yes, of course, but you're not like the rest of them, Your Majesty; you wouldn't rob a poor little old woman like me!'

'Bilberries; that's what I want!' said the bear, and put his head down to start eating.

In a flash Mrs Pepperpot had jumped on his neck and started tickling him behind his ear.

'What are you doing?' asked the bear.

'I'm just tickling your ears for you,' answered Mrs Pepperpot. 'Doesn't it feel good?'

'Good? It's almost better than eating the berries!' said the bear.

'Well, if Your Majesty would be so kind as to carry the bucket, I could be tickling Your Majesty's ears all the way,' said the artful Mrs Pepperpot.

'Oh, very well then,' grumbled the bear.

When they reached the road the bear put the bucket down very carefully on a flat stone.

'Many, many thanks, Your Majesty,' said Mrs Pepperpot as she made another deep curtsey.

'Thank *you*,' said the bear, and shuffled off into the forest.

When the bear had gone Mrs Pepperpot became her usual size again, so she picked up her bucket and hurried homeward.

'It's really not very difficult to look after yourself, even when you're only the size of a pepperpot,' she told herself. 'As long as you know how to tackle the people you meet. Cunning people must be tricked, cowardly ones must be frightened, and the big, strong ones must have their ears tickled.'

As for bad-tempered husbands, the only thing to do with *them* is to give them bilberry jam with their pancakes.

Mrs Pepperpot minds the baby

Now I'll tell you what happened the day Mrs Pepperpot was asked to mind the baby.

It was early in the morning. Mrs Pepperpot had sent her husband off to work. In the usual way wives do, she had made the coffee and the sandwiches for his lunch, and had stood by the window and waved till he was out of sight. Then, just like other wives, she had gone back to bed to have a little extra shut-eye, leaving all her housework for later.

She had been sleeping a couple of hours when there was a knock at the door. She looked at the clock. 'Good heavens!' she cried, 'have I slept so long?' She pulled her clothes on very quickly and ran to open the door.

In the porch stood a lady with a little boy on her arm.

'Forgive me for knocking,' said the lady.

'You're welcome,' said Mrs Pepperpot.

'You see,' said the lady, 'I'm staying with my aunt near here with my little boy, and today we simply *have* to go shopping in the town. I can't take Roger and there's no one in the house to look after him.'

'Oh, that's all right!' said Mrs Pepperpot. 'I'll look after your little boy.' (To herself she thought: 'However will I manage with all that work and me oversleeping like that. Ah well, I shall have to do both at the same time.') Then she said out loud: 'Roger, come to Mrs Pepperpot? That's right!' And she took the baby from the lady.

'You don't need to give him a meal,' said the lady. 'I've brought some apples he can have when he starts sucking his fingers.'

'Very well,' said Mrs Pepperpot, and put the apples in a dish on the sideboard.

The lady said good-bye and Mrs Pepperpot set the baby down on the rug in the sitting-room. Then she went out into the kitchen to fetch her broom to start sweeping up. At that very moment she *shrank*!

'Oh dear! Oh dear! Whatever shall I do?' she wailed, for of course now she was much smaller than the baby. She gave up any idea of cleaning the house; when her husband came home she would have to tell him that she had had a headache.

'I must go and see what that little fellow is doing,' she thought, as she climbed over the doorstep into the sitting-room. Not a moment too soon! For Roger had crawled right across the floor and was just about to pull the tablecloth off the table together with a pot of jam, a loaf of bread, and a big jug of coffee!

Mrs Pepperpot lost no time. She knew it was too far for her to get to the table, so she pushed over a large silver cup which was standing on the floor, waiting to be polished. Her husband had won it years ago when he was young in a skiing competition.

The cup made a fine booming noise as it fell; the baby turned round and started crawling towards it.

'That's right,' said Mrs Pepperpot, 'you play with that; at least you can't break it.'

But Roger wasn't after the silver cup. Gurgling: 'Ha' dolly! Ha' dolly!' he made a bee-line for Mrs Pepperpot, and before she could get away, he had grabbed her by the waist! He jogged her up and down and every time Mrs Pepperpot kicked and wriggled to get free, he laughed. ' 'Ickle, 'ickle!' he shouted, for she was tickling his hand with her feet.

'Let go! Let go!' yelled Mrs Pepperpot. But Roger was used to his father shouting 'Let's go!' when he threw him up in the air and caught him again. So Roger shouted 'Leggo! Leggo!' and threw the little old woman up in the air with all the strength of his short arms. Mrs Pepperpot went up and up – nearly to the ceiling! Luckily she

landed on the sofa, but she bounced several times before she could stop.

'Talk of flying through the air with the greatest of ease!' she gasped. 'If that had happened to me in my normal size I'd most likely have broken every bone in my body. Ah well, I'd better see what my little friend is up to now.'

She soon found out. Roger had got hold of a matchbox and was trying to strike a match.

Luckily he was using the wrong side of the box, but Mrs Pepperpot had to think very quickly indeed.

'Youngsters like to copy everything you do, so I'll take this nut and throw it at him. Then he'll throw it at me – I hope.'

She had found the nut in the sofa and now she was in such a hurry to throw it she forgot to aim properly. But it was a lucky shot and it hit Roger just behind the ear, making him turn round. 'What else can I throw?' wondered Mrs Pepperpot, but there was no need, because the baby had seen her; he dropped the match-box and started crawling towards the sofa.

'Ha' dolly! Ha' dolly!' he gurgled delightedly. And now they started a very funny game of hide-and-seek – at least it was fun for Roger, but not quite so amusing for poor little old Mrs Pepperpot who had to hide behind the cushions to get away from him. In the end she managed to climb on to the sideboard where she kept a precious geranium in a pot.

'Aha, you can't catch me now!' she said, feeling much safer.

But at that moment the baby decided to go back to the match-box. 'No, no, no!' shouted Mrs

Pepperpot. Roger took no notice. So, when she saw he was trying to strike another match, she put her back against the flowerpot and gave it a push so that it fell to the floor with a crash.

Roger immediately left the match-box for this new and interesting mess of earth and bits of broken flowerpot. He buried both his hands in it and started putting it in his mouth, gurgling, 'Nice din-din!'

'No, no, no!' shouted Mrs Pepperpot once more. 'Oh, whatever shall I do?' Her eye caught the apples left by Roger's mother. They were right beside her on the dish. One after the other she rolled them over the edge of the dish on to the floor. Roger watched them roll, then he decided to chase them, forgetting his lovely meal of earth and broken flowerpot. Soon the apples were all over the floor and the baby was crawling happily from one to the other.

There was a knock on the door.

'Come in,' said Mrs Pepperpot.

Roger's mother opened the door and came in, and there was Mrs Pepperpot as large as life, carrying a dustpan full of earth and broken bits in one hand and her broom in the other.

'Has he been naughty?' asked the lady.

'As good as gold,' said Mrs Pepperpot. 'We've had a high old time together, haven't we, Roger?' And she handed him back to his mother.

'I'll have to take you home now, precious,' said the lady.

But the little fellow began to cry. 'Ha' dolly! Ha' dolly!' he sobbed.

'Have *dolly*?' said his mother. 'But you didn't bring a dolly – you don't even have one at home.' She turned to Mrs Pepperpot. 'I don't know what he means.'

'Oh, children say so many things grown-ups don't understand,' said Mrs Pepperpot, and waved good-bye to Roger and his mother.

Then she set about cleaning up her house.

The good luck story

ONCE upon a time there was a little old woman – no, what am I saying? She was a little girl. But this little girl worked every bit as hard as any grown-up woman. Her name was Betsy; she wore a scarf round her head like the women did, and she could weed a field of turnips with the best of them. If any of the big boys started throwing stones or lumps of earth at her, she tossed her head and gave them a piece of her mind.

She was weeding in the field one day when a ladybird settled on her hand.

'Poor little ladybird! What do you want on my thumb?' said Betsy, at the same time trying to think of a really good wish. For ever since she was tiny she had been told to make a wish when a ladybird flew from her finger.

'I wish ... I wish I had a new skipping-rope to take to school,' she said quickly. But then she remembered that she had borrowed a skipping-rope from her friend, Anna, and lost it. If she got a new one now she would *have* to give it to Anna.

The ladybird crawled slowly out on Betsy's thumb-nail, and she was terrified it would fly away before she had had time to wish for all the things she wanted. Luckily, the ladybird changed its mind when it reached the top; it crawled down again and started up the first finger.

'Now I shall wish – I wish I could have some

money,' said Betsy, but was sorry as soon as she had said it. After all, she would *get* some money when she had finished her weeding. And, anyway, the money would have to go to Britta from Hill Farm to pay for the old bicycle Betsy had bought from her in the spring.

The ladybird crawled right out on the top of Betsy's first finger. Then it stopped to consider, and slowly turned round and climbed down again to start on the second finger.

'Now I must hurry up and wish before it flies off the top of this finger,' said Betsy, while the lady-bird climbed steadily upwards.

'I wish I were a real princess,' she said, but then she thought: 'How stupid of me – how can I be a real princess if I haven't been one before? Unless, of course, a prince came along and asked me to marry him. That would look funny, wouldn't it? A prince in a turnip field!' And she laughed at herself.

The ladybird was stretching one wing now and hovering.

'Don't fly yet, little ladybird! I don't want to be a princess at all. I want something quite different. I want my mother to be rid of her rheumatics when I get home tonight.'

This was a good wish, and Betsy was pleased with it. You see, it was a great trouble to her when her mother had the rheumatics; then Betsy had to dress all her little brothers and sisters and give them their dinner. It would be nice not to have to work so hard.

But the ladybird didn't take off even from this finger. Slowly it turned round and made its way to the bottom of the finger and then on to Betsy's hand. Then it stopped; it didn't seem to want to go on at all. But Betsy gave it a gentle little push and got it on to her third finger.

Now she knew what to wish; that her father could get the job he was after that day. Because if he did, he had said he would buy her a whole sheet of pictures to stick in her scrap-book.

But the ladybird had its own ideas; it crawled more and more slowly up Betsy's third finger, and every now and then Betsy had to poke it to get it out on the nail. Then all of a sudden the ladybird rolled off and fell on to the ground.

Betsy lay down flat among the turnips and managed to coax the creature on to her little finger. It didn't move. So Betsy lifted it gingerly out on the nail. Still it didn't move, and she thought she must have hurt it. 'You poor thing! Did I squeeze you too hard? Oh, please, little ladybird, do fly now! Because I want to wish that Daddy could get the job he's after!'

And suddenly the ladybird opened its wings and flew off – straight up towards the sun.

And do you know? When Betsy got home that night her mother was feeling better than she had been for a long while. Her father had got the job and had remembered the pictures for her scrap-book, and her friend Anna had been to see her. She had found the lost skipping-rope and brought it for Betsy, because she had a new one herself. Not only that, but Britta from Hill Farm had been to say that if Betsy would mind her baby for her twice that week, she needn't pay any more for the old bicycle!

What more could you want from a lucky lady-bird?

Mr Big Toe's journey

MR BIG TOE lived with his four brothers in a little sock, and the sock lived in a shoe which belonged to a little boy who was walking down the lane eating a very big sandwich.

Mr Big Toe said: 'Now I've been stuck in this place so long, I think it's time I did some travelling.'

When his brothers asked him where he was going, he answered: 'Oh, I expect I shall sail across the ocean.'

'But how will you get through the wall?' they asked him – they meant the sock, of course.

'That's easy for someone as big as I am. I shall just scratch a hole.'

'Will we never see you again?' asked the one who was closest to Mr Big Toe.

'Maybe not. But I'll ring you up and tell you how I'm getting on. Well, I'm off now, so good-bye!'

Then Mr Big Toe started scratching a hole, and it didn't take long before he had wriggled through.

The rest of the toes sat waiting for the telephone message.

Soon the little boy started running and Mr Big Toe sent his first message:

'Hullo, hullo! I've started on my travels. It feels a bit strange at first, of course, and I miss you a bit. But I expect you miss me much more. Be good. I'll ring you up again when I get on the boat.'

After a time the little boy found a puddle and began dipping his shoe in it. Mr Big Toe got on the telephone again.

'Hullo boys, I've just got to the edge of the ocean; in a few moments I'll be sailing to the far shore. It's a dangerous journey, but don't worry, I'll manage! The waves are enormous! Still, the boat seems strong and seaworthy. It won't be long now before I meet the African Chief's Big Toe and all his little black brothers. I'll tell them I've left *my* four brothers at home. They'll be glad to hear about you, I expect. ... Bye, bye, I must ring off now till we get to the far shore.'

The boy waded out into the middle of the puddle, but it was deeper than he thought, and while the other toes were lying inside the sock, thinking of their big brother alone on the stormy sea, they had another call from him.

'Hullo there! This is getting more and more dangerous; the boat is out in the middle of the ocean, and it's leaking badly. If you don't hear anything more for a bit, it's because I have to use my nail to bail the water out. It's difficult, but I'm not a bit afraid!'

'Poor Big Toe!' the brothers said to each other and huddled closer together inside the sock.

The little boy had splashed through the puddle by now. Next he found a tricycle and got on it. He rode it as fast as he could and stuck both his legs straight out in the air.

Mr Big Toe's telephone rang again. 'Hullo boys, hullo! It's your brother Big Toe calling. I'm floating in mid-air. I'm in an aeroplane, but you needn't worry, it's quite safe. The boat sank, though I did my best to bail all the water out. I was alone, you see, that made it very difficult. However, you'll be pleased to know I'm on my way home now. See you all soon!'

The boy went indoors to change his wet socks. The five toes got a new home to live in and the boy set out again with another big sandwich in his hand.

'Fancy you coming home to us!' said all the brothers to Mr Big Toe, and they curled themselves round him to make him feel warm and cosy.

'Yes, yes, home is all right when the sock is dry and clean,' said Mr Big Toe. 'But I don't suppose it will be long before I take another journey.'

A birthday party
in Topsy Turvy Town

In Topsy Turvy Town, where the sun rises in the West and goes down in the North, and three times fourteen is four, the Mayor was going to have his fiftieth birthday. His little girl, Trixie, was busy baking cakes, but she couldn't get on, because the Mayor *would* keep bothering her to know how much longer it would be before his birthday.

'Do stop bothering me, Daddy dear,' she said. 'When you've slept one more night it will be your birthday. So run along to your office now, please, and write out invitations to the people you want to come to your party.'

'I won't ask the Postmaster, anyway,' said the Mayor.

'Why ever not?'

'He always teases me about my big ears,' answered the Mayor.

'That's only when he's with the Smith,' said

Trixie. 'You always play perfectly well when the Smith isn't there.'

'But I want to ask the Smith,' said the Mayor. 'I'm sure he'll behave if he knows we're having birthday cake.'

'Well, you'd better ask them both, then.'

'I want to ask the Doctor and the Dentist as well,' said the Mayor.

'I only hope the Doctor will be well enough to go out,' said Trixie. 'I spoke to his little girl yester-

day, and she told me he had had a very bad night, tossing and turning. She was afraid he might be sickening for something. But I expect you'd better ask him all the same.'

'Oh yes, otherwise he'd sulk,' said the Mayor. 'So would the Dentist.'

'You do as you like,' said Trixie, 'but you know he isn't allowed any sweet things like chocolate cake with icing on.'

'I know. But we could give him apples and rusks instead,' said the Mayor.

'That's a good idea. Are you asking any more?'

'What a question! I can't leave the Baker out, can I?'

'Now, now, that's not the way for a Mayor to talk to his little girl!' said Trixie. 'Anyway, if you ask him you can't have any more; there isn't room.' Then she told him to put the invitations through the letter-boxes and come straight home to bed to have a good sleep before the great day.

*   *   *

The next day the Mayor was very excited. He sat in his office and looked at the clock till it was time to go home. Then he raced back to put on his

Grand Chain of Office and went and stood by the door to welcome his guests

The first to arrive was the Smith. He had his hands in his pockets.

'Many Happy Returns of the Day,' he said.

'Thank you,' said the Mayor, holding out his hand for the present.

'Haven't brought a present,' said the Smith.

'Never mind,' said Trixie soothingly. 'Wouldn't you like to take off those big heavy boots before you come in?'

'No,' said the Smith.

'Why not?' asked the little girl.

'Hole in my sock,' said the Smith.

'You can borrow my daddy's slippers. And then what about taking your hands out of your pockets?'

'No,' said the Smith.

'Why not?'

'Dirty,' said the Smith.

'Oh, we'll soon deal with that!' said Trixie. 'You come along to the bathroom with me; I'll help you wash them. You'll have to let the others in by yourself, Daddy dear.'

Next came the Doctor and the Dentist. They walked hand-in-hand and each had a little parcel under his arm.

'Many Happy Returns,' they said, both together.

'Thank you very much,' said the Mayor, and started unwrapping. The Doctor's present was a stethoscope, but it was only a toy, because it was broken. The Dentist gave him a nice thing to squirt his mouth with.

Then came the Postmaster, and he brought a packet of stamps which were very unusual, because all the edges had been cut off.

Last of all came the Baker. He brought a large slab of chocolate, and when he had wished the Mayor many happy returns he broke the chocolate in two, gave one half to the Mayor and stuffed the other half in his pocket.

'Come in, all of you,' Trixie said, as she came out of the bathroom with the Smith. His hands were now so clean, he was ashamed to show them.

In the dining-room there was a fine spread, with a huge birthday cake in the middle of the table decorated with fifty candles.

'Now do sit down and help yourselves,' invited Trixie. 'I'm just going to telephone.' And she shut the door. She picked up the receiver. 'Hullo, can you please give me the little girl in Flat 2?'

'There you are,' said the operator.

'Hullo, is that you, Kitty? This is Trixie.'

'Oh, hullo Trixie! What do you want?'

'Could you come and help me this afternoon? My daddy is having a birthday party and there *is* so much to do!'

'Yes, all right. But I'll have to bring my doll's ironing; there's a whole heap of it,' said Kitty on the telephone.

'We can iron together, then. *I* have a whole heap to do as well,' said Trixie.

As she put the phone down, Trixie heard a terrible crash from the dining-room, and when she opened the door what a sight met her eyes! There was birthday cake plastered all over the walls, and cups and saucers were strewn about the floor!

'What is the meaning of this?' she demanded sternly.

It was the Postmaster who answered. 'Well, you see, the Mayor tried to blow out the candles and he couldn't do it, so we all had a go and none of us could do it. Except the Smith.'

Trixie frowned. 'How did *you* manage it when the others couldn't do it?' she asked.

'Had my bellows,' said the Smith, staring up at the ceiling.

'Oh dear,' sighed Trixie. 'I suppose I shall have to clean up the mess. But then you really must behave. I have someone coming to see me, and we shall be in the nursery. So you're not to come in there. You can play in the sitting-room when you have finished your tea.' Then she left them to get on with it.

*　　　*　　　*

Trixie and her friend Kitty were ironing their dolls' clothes and having a very interesting talk together when suddenly there was another awful crash from the room where the party was going on. The Mayor came and knocked on the nursery door.

'What is it?' asked Trixie.

'It's the Postmaster,' said the Mayor; 'he's started teasing me again; I want him to go home.'

Trixie had to go and make peace. 'I really don't

know why you can't play nicely instead of quarrel-ling,' she said.

The Postmaster was standing next to the Smith, staring at the floor. The Smith was looking at the ceiling, as usual.

'What did the Postmaster say?' asked Trixie.

'He said my ears were so big he would put a stamp on my forehead and send me by air-mail,' said the Mayor.

'*We* never put stamps on people and send them by air-mail,' said the Doctor and the Dentist, both together.

'Oh, how silly!' said Trixie. 'Now please be good boys and play a game, or something. What about Blind Man's Buff? Then I'll go and cook some lovely hot sausages for you.'

Trixie called to Kitty. 'I'll have to stop ironing dolls' clothes now, I must cook the sausages.'

'I'll come and help you,' said Kitty. 'I've finished my ironing.'

'Good,' said Trixie. But no sooner had they got to work in the kitchen when the door of the sitting-room flew open, and the Baker rushed out, grabbing his coat from the peg. Then he shot through the front door and down the main stairs, taking two at a time.

'*Now* what's happened?' asked Trixie.

The Mayor, who was nearly crying, came out in the kitchen. 'The Baker snatched his present back and ran off, just because he couldn't catch any of us in Blind Man's Buff,' he said.

'Oh dear! Oh dear!' said Trixie.

'*We* don't snatch our presents back and run off home,' said the Doctor and the Dentist.

'Of course not. You're *good* boys,' said Trixie, 'and I have some nice hot sausages for you.' Suddenly she noticed the Dentist's face. 'Goodness

Gracious!' she exclaimed. 'What's that swelling you have on your cheek?' She beckoned to Kitty to have a look. 'I do believe he's got an ab – ab – what's it called?'

'You mean an abscess,' said Kitty, who was very clever. She climbed on the Dentist's knee. The Dentist opened his mouth wide, and, sure enough, he had an abscess!

'You'll have to go home to your little girl at once,' said Trixie, 'and get her to pull out the tooth for you.'

'He's not the only one who'll have to go home,' said Kitty. 'Look at the Doctor, he's coming out in spots all over his face. I expect he's getting measles.'

'Goodness Gracious!' cried Trixie. 'You'll all have to go at once before you catch the measles. Hurry and get your things on!'

So they all put on their coats and shook hands and said 'thank you' before they went home.

All except the Smith. He sat in the hall and took a very long time to put on his boots.

'You must go home to *your* little girl now,' said Trixie.

'Haven't got one,' said the Smith, with his eyes on the ceiling.

Trixie and Kitty both said 'Oh, you poor thing!' and they gave him all that was left of the birthday cake and a whole bucket, full of sausages, to take home.

The Mayor walked round the dining-room table, scraping all the plates and drinking all the cold tea. He thought it had been a wonderful party.

Mrs Pepperpot's penny watchman

STRANGE things had been happening in Mrs Pepperpot's house. It all began when a little girl came to the door selling penny raffle tickets for a tablecloth. Mrs Pepperpot hunted high and low until she found a penny; it was a nice shiny one, because someone had been polishing it. But just as she was writing her name on the ticket, the penny dropped on the floor and rolled into a crack by the trapdoor to the cellar.

'Bang goes my fortune,' said Mrs Pepperpot, as she watched it disappear. 'Now I won't be able to buy a raffle ticket after all. But I can't let you go without giving you anything; what about a nice home-made short-cake?' And she stood on a stool to reach the cake-tin.

It was empty. Mrs Pepperpot turned the tin almost inside out, but there was no sign of any short-cake.

'I can't understand it,' she said. 'I baked two whole rounds of short-cake on Friday. Today it's only Monday, and the tin is empty. Very

mysterious. But I've got something you might like even better, little girl.' So saying, Mrs Pepperpot opened the trapdoor to the cellar and climbed down the ladder to fetch the big jar of bramble jelly she had left over from the summer.

But what a sight met her eyes!

'Goodness Gracious and Glory Be!' she exclaimed, for the big jar of bramble jelly was lying smashed under the shelf with the jelly gently oozing out over the floor. From the sticky mess a little trail of mouse footprints ran across to the chimney.

There was nothing for it – Mrs Pepperpot had to go up to the little girl and tell her she couldn't even have bramble jelly. But the little girl said it

didn't matter a bit and politely curtsied before going on to the next house.

Mrs Pepperpot took a mouse-trap and went
down the cellar steps again. She baited it with
cheese and set it very carefully on the floor. When
it was done she turned to go upstairs again, but
the hem of her skirt brushed against it, and SNAP!
went the trap, with a corner of her skirt caught in
it. That was bad enough, but then, if you please,
she shrank again!

'Now I really *am* stuck!' she told herself, and

she certainly was; she couldn't move an inch. After she had sat there a while she saw a young mouse peeping over the edge of an empty flower-pot.

'You're quite safe to come out,' said Mrs Pepperpot. 'I'm too well tethered to do you any harm at the moment.'

But the little mouse darted off to an empty card-

board box and then two little mice popped their noses over the edge.

'One and one makes two,' said Mrs Pepperpot. 'I learned that at school, and I wouldn't be a bit surprised if you fetched a third one – for one and two make three!'

She was right. The two little mice darted off to-gether and stayed away quite a long time while she sat and waited. Suddenly she heard a tinny little sound. Ping! Ping! And a big mouse came walking towards her on his hind legs, banging a shiny gong with a little steel pin. The shiny gong was Mrs Pepperpot's lost penny!

The big mouse bowed low. 'Queen of the House, I greet you!' The little mice were peeping out from behind him.

'Thank goodness for that!' said Mrs Pepperpot. 'For a moment I thought you might be coming to gobble me up – you're so much bigger than I am!'

'We're not in the habit of gobbling up queens,' said the large mouse. 'I just wanted to tell you, you have a thief in your house.'

Mrs Pepperpot snorted. 'Thief indeed! Of course I have; you and all the other mice are the thieves in my house. Whose penny is it you're using for a gong, may I ask?'

'Oh, is that what it is? A penny?' said the big mouse. 'Well, it rolled through a crack in the floor, you see, so I thought I could use it to scare away the thief and to show I'm the watchman in this house. You really do need a watchman, Queen of the House, to keep an eye on things for you.'

'What nonsense!' said Mrs Pepperpot. She

tried to stand up, but it was rather difficult with her dress caught in the trap and she herself so tiny.

'Take it easy, Queen of the House,' said the big mouse. 'Let my son here tell you what he has seen.'

Timidly, one of the little mice came forward and told how he had climbed up the chimney one day and peeped through a hole into the kitchen. There he had seen a terrible monster who was eating up all the cake in the tin.

Then the other little mouse chirped in to tell how he had been playing hide-and-seek behind a jam-jar on the shelf when the monster had put out a huge hand and taken the jar away. But he had been so scared when he saw the little mouse that he had dropped the jar on the floor, and all the bramble jelly came pouring out.

Suddenly they heard Tramp! Tramp! Tramp! up above; the sound of huge boots walking about.

'That's the monster!' said one of the little mice.

'Yes, that's him all right!' said the other little mouse.

'Is it, indeed!' said Mrs Pepperpot. 'If only I

could get out of this trap, I should very much like to go and have a look at this monster.'

'We'll help you,' said all the mice, and they set to work to free Mrs Pepperpot from the trap in the way only mice know how; they gnawed through her skirt, leaving a piece stuck in the spring.

'Now you must hurry up to the kitchen to see the monster,' they said.

'But how am I to get there?' asked Mrs Pepperpot.

'Up through the chimney on our special rope; we'll pull you up.'

And that's what they did. They hoisted Mrs Pepperpot higher and higher inside the chimney, until she could see a chink of light.

'That's the crack into the kitchen,' the big mouse told her from below.

She called down to him: 'Thank you Mr Watchman, thank you for your help, and keep a sharp look-out!' Then she climbed through the hole in the wall. As soon as she set foot on the floor she grew to her normal size. Standing in front of the stove, she put her hands on her hips, and said, 'So it's you, husband, is it, who's been eating all my short-cake and stealing the bramble jelly in the cellar?'

Mr Pepperpot looked dumbfounded: 'How did you know that?' he said.

'Because I have a watchman now, I have paid him a penny,' said Mrs Pepperpot.

Mrs Pepperpot finds a
hidden treasure

IT was a fine sunny day in January, and Mrs
Pepperpot was peeling potatoes at the kitchen
sink.

'Miaow!' said the cat; she was lying in front of
the stove.

'Miaow yourself!' answered Mrs Pepperpot.

'Miaow!' said the cat again.

Mrs Pepperpot suddenly remembered an old,
old rhyme she learned when she was a child. It
went like this:

> *The cat sat by the fire,*
> *Her aches and pains were dire,*
> *Such throbbing in my head,*
> *She cried; I'll soon be dead!*

'Poor Pussy! Are your aches and pains so bad?
Does your head throb?' she said, and smiled down
at the cat.

But the cat only looked at her.

Mrs Pepperpot stopped peeling potatoes, wiped her hands, and knelt down beside the cat. 'There's something you want to tell me, isn't there, Pussy? It's too bad I can't understand you except when I'm little, but it's not my fault.' She stroked the cat, but Pussy didn't purr, just went on looking at her.

'Well, I can't spend all day being sorry for you, my girl, I've got a husband to feed,' said Mrs Pepperpot, and went back to the potatoes in the sink. When they were ready she put them in a saucepan of cold water on the stove, not forgetting a good pinch of salt. After that she laid the table, for her husband had to have his dinner sharp at one o'clock and it was now half past twelve.

Pussy was at the door now. 'Miaow!' she said, scratching at it.

'You want to get out, do you?' said Mrs Pepperpot, and opened the door. She followed the cat out, because she had noticed that her broom had fallen over in the snow. The door closed behind her.

And at that moment she shrank to her pepperpot size!

'About time too!' said the cat. 'I've been waiting for days for this to happen. Now don't let's waste any more time; jump on my back! We're setting off at once.'

Mrs Pepperpot didn't stop to ask where they were going; she climbed on Pussy's back. 'Hold on tight!' said Pussy, and bounded off down the little bank at the back of the house past Mrs Pepperpot's rubbish-heap.

'We're coming to the first hindrance,' said Pussy; 'just sit tight and don't say a word!' All Mrs Pepperpot could see was a single birch-tree with a couple of magpies on it. True, the birds seemed as big as eagles to her now and the tree was like a mountain. But when the magpies started screeching she knew what the cat meant.

'There's the cat! There's the cat!' they screamed. 'Let's nip her tail! Let's pull her whiskers!' And they swooped down, skimming so close over Mrs Pepperpot's head she was nearly blown off the cat's back. But the cat took no notice at all, just kept steadily on down the hill, and the magpies soon tired of the game.

'That's that!' said the cat. 'The next thing we have to watch out for is being hit by snowballs. We have to cross the boys' playground now, so if

any of them start aiming at you, duck behind my ears and hang on!'

Mrs Pepperpot looked at the boys; she knew them all, she had often given them sweets and biscuits. '*They* can't be dangerous,' she said to herself.

But then she heard one of them say: 'There comes that stupid cat; let's see who can hit it first! Come on, boys!' And they all started pelting snowballs as hard as they could.

Suddenly remembering how small she was, Mrs Pepperpot did as the cat had told her and crouched down behind Pussy's ears until they were safely out of range.

The cat ran on till they got to a wire fence with a hole just big enough for her to wriggle through.

'So far, so good,' she said, 'but now comes the worst bit, because this is dog land, and we don't want to get caught. So keep your eyes skinned!'

The fence divided Mrs Pepperpot's land from her neighbour's, but she knew the neighbour's dog quite well; he had had many a bone and scraps from her and he was always very friendly. 'We'll be all right here,' she thought.

But she was wrong. Without any warning, that

dog suddenly came bearing down on them in great leaps and bounds! Mrs Pepperpot shook like a jelly when she saw his wide-open jaws all red, with sharp, white teeth glistening in a terrifying way. She flattened herself on the cat's back and clung on for dear life, for Pussy shot like a Sputnik across the yard and straight under the neighbour's barn.

'Phew!' said the cat, 'that was a narrow squeak! Thanks very much for coming all this way with me; I'm afraid it wasn't a very comfortable journey.'

'That's all right,' said Mrs Pepperpot, 'but perhaps you'll tell me now what we've come for?'

'It's a surprise,' said Pussy, 'but don't worry, you'll get your reward. All we have to do now is to find the hidden treasure, but that means crawling through the hay. So hang on!'

And off they went again, slowly this time, for it

was difficult to make their way through the prickly stalks that seemed as big as bean-poles to Mrs Pepperpot. The dust was terrible; it went in her eyes, her mouth, her hair, down her neck – everywhere.

'Can you see anything?' asked the cat.

'Only blackness,' answered Mrs Pepperpot, 'and it seems to be getting blacker.'

'In that case we're probably going the right way,' said Pussy, crawling further into the hay. 'D'you see anything now?' she asked.

'Nothing at all,' said Mrs Pepperpot, for by now her eyes were completely bunged up with hay-seed and dust.

'Try rubbing your eyes,' said the cat, 'for this is where your hidden treasure is.'

So Mrs Pepperpot rubbed her eyes, blinked, and rubbed again until at last she could open them properly. When she did, she was astonished; all round her shone the most wonderful jewels! Diamonds, sapphires, emeralds – they glittered in every hue!

'There you are! Didn't I tell you I had a hidden treasure for you?' said the cat, but she didn't give Mrs Pepperpot time to have a closer look.

'We'll have to hurry back now, it's nearly time for your husband's dinner.'

So they crawled back through the hay and, just as they got out in the daylight, Mrs Pepperpot grew to her ordinary size. She picked the cat up in her arms and walked across the yard with her. The dog was there, but what a different dog! He nuzzled Mrs Pepperpot's skirt and wagged his tail in the friendliest way.

Through the gate they came to the place where the boys were playing. Every one of them nodded to her and politely said 'Good morning.' Then they went on up the hill, and there were the magpies in the birch-tree. But not a sound came from them; they didn't even seem to notice them walking by.

When they got to the house Mrs Pepperpot put the cat down and hurried indoors. It was almost one o'clock. She snatched the saucepan from the stove – a few potatoes had stuck to the bottom, so she threw those out and emptied the rest into a blue serving-bowl. The saucepan she put outside the back door with cold water in it.

She had only just got everything ready when Mr Pepperpot came in. He sniffed suspiciously. 'I can smell burnt potatoes,' he said.

'Nonsense,' said Mrs Pepperpot, 'I dropped a bit of potato-skin on the stove, that's all. But I've aired the room since, so just you sit down and eat your dinner.'

'Aren't you having any?' asked her husband.

'Not just now,' answered Mrs Pepperpot, 'I have to go and fetch something first. I won't be long.' And Mrs Pepperpot went back down the hill, through the gate to her neighbour's yard, and into the barn. But this time she climbed *over* the hay till she found the spot where her hidden treasure lay.

And what d'you think it was?

Four coal-black kittens with shining eyes!

Mr Pepperpot

Now you have heard a lot about *Mrs* Pepperpot, but hardly anything about *Mr* Pepperpot.

He usually comes in at the end of the stories, when Mrs Pepperpot is back to her normal size and busy with his dinner. If the food isn't ready he always says 'Can't a man ever get his dinner at the proper time in this house?' And if it is ready, he just sits down to eat and says nothing at all. If it's cold out, he says 'Brrrrrrr!' and if it's very hot, he says 'Pheeew!' If Mrs Pepperpot has done something he doesn't like, he says 'Hmmmmm!' in a disapproving tone of voice. But if he himself is thinking of doing something he doesn't want Mrs Pepperpot to know about, he goes round the house whistling to himself and humming a little tune.

One evening when he came home, he went up to the attic. Now, Mrs Pepperpot had hidden four black kittens up there, because Mr Pepperpot didn't like kittens when they were small (some people don't, you know). So, when Mr Pepperpot came down from the attic, he stood in the middle of the floor and said 'Hmmmmm!' And a little later he started whistling and humming his little tune.

Mrs Pepperpot said nothing, though she knew what it meant. She just took his old winter coat from its peg and started mending a tear in it.

'What are you mending that for?' asked Mr Pepperpot.

'The weather's getting so bad, you'll need it,' said Mrs Pepperpot.

'Who said I was going out?' asked Mr Pepperpot.

'You can do as you like,' said his wife, 'I'm staying right where I am.'

'Well, maybe I *will* take a turn outside, all the same,' said Mr Pepperpot.

'I thought you would,' she said.

Mr Pepperpot went back to the attic, found a big sack and popped the four kittens inside. But when he got to the bottom of the stairs, he thought he would put on the old winter coat. So he let the sack down and went into the kitchen. There he found the coat hanging over a chair.

'I'm going out now!' he called, thinking his wife must be in the sitting-room. He got no answer, but he didn't bother to call again, as he was afraid the kittens might get out of the sack which wasn't properly tied. Quickly he slung it over his shoulder and went out.

It was a nasty night; the wind blew sleet in his face and the road was full of icy puddles.

'Ugh!' said Mr Pepperpot, 'this weather's fit to drown in!'

'Isn't that just what you're going to do to us poor kittens?' said a tiny voice close by.

Mr Pepperpot was startled. 'Who said that, I wonder?' he said. He put the sack down to look inside, but as soon as he opened it out jumped one of the kittens and ran off in the darkness.

'Oh dear, what shall I do?' he said, tying up the sack again as quickly as he could. 'I can't leave a kitten running about on a night like this.'

'He won't get any wetter than the rest of us by the time you've finished with us,' said the little voice again.

Mr Pepperpot untied the sack once more to find out who was speaking. Out jumped the second kitten and disappeared in the sleet and snow. While he hurriedly tied a knot to stop the rest from getting out, he said to himself:

'What if the fox got those two little mites? That would be terrible!'

'No worse than being in *your* hands,' said the tiny voice.

This time, Mr Pepperpot was very careful to hold his hand over the opening as he untied it. But his foot slipped on the ice and jogged the sack out of his hand, and another kitten got away.

'Three gone! That's bad!' he said.

'Not as bad as it'll be for me!' came the voice from the sack.

'I know who it is now,' said Mr Pepperpot: 'it's

my old woman who's shrunk again. You're in that sack, aren't you? But I'll catch you! You just wait!' And with that he opened the sack again.

Out jumped the fourth kitten and ran off, lickety-split!

'You can run, I don't care!' said the old man. 'I'm going to catch that wife of mine – it's all her fault!' He got down on his knees and rummaged round in every corner of the sack. But he found nothing – it was quite empty.

Now he really was worried; he was so worried he started sobbing and crying, and in between he called 'Puss, Puss!' and searched all over the place.

A little girl came along the road. 'What have you lost?' she asked.

'Some kittens,' sniffed Mr Pepperpot.

'I'll help you find them,' said the little girl.

Soon they were joined by a little boy, and he had a torch which made it easier to search. First the little girl found one kitten behind a tree-stump, then the boy found two kittens stuck in a snow-drift, and Mr Pepperpot himself found the fourth one and put them all back in the sack, tying it very securely this time.

'Thank you for your help,' he said to the children and asked them to take the kittens back to his house and put them in the kitchen.

When they had gone, he started looking for his little old woman. He searched for an hour – for two hours; he called, he begged, he sobbed, he was quite beside himself. But in the end he had to give up. 'I'll go home now,' he said to himself, 'and try again tomorrow.'

But when he got home, there was Mrs Pepperpot, as large as life, bustling round the kitchen, frying a huge pile of pancakes! And by the kitchen stove was a wicker basket with the mother cat and all four kittens in it.

'When did you come home?' asked the astonished Mr Pepperpot.

'When did I come home? Why, I've been here all the time, of course,' she said.

'But who was it talking to me from the sack, then?'

'I've no idea,' said Mrs Pepperpot, 'unless it was your conscience.' And she came over and gave him a great big hug and kiss.

Then Mr Pepperpot sat down to eat the biggest pile of pancakes he had ever had and all with bilberry jam, and when he was full the kittens finished off the last four.

And after that Mr and Mrs Pepperpot lived happily together, and Mrs Pepperpot gave up shrinking for a very long time indeed.

Some other Young Puffins

LUCKY DIP *Ruth Ainsworth*
ANOTHER LUCKY DIP
Stories from the BBC's *Listen With Mother*. Some of the ever-popular *Charles* stories are included.

THE TEN TALES OF SHELLOVER *Ruth Ainsworth*
The Black Hens, the Dog and the Cat didn't like Shellover the tortoise at first, until they discovered what wonderful stories he told.

MY FIRST BIG STORY BOOK *ed. Richard Bamberger*
MY SECOND BIG STORY BOOK
MY THIRD BIG STORY BOOK
A wonderful hoard of nursery rhymes and bed-time stories, ranging from traditional English favourites to strange new tales from other lands.

TALES FROM THE END COTTAGE *Eileen Bell*
MORE TALES FROM THE END COTTAGE
Two tabby cats and a peke live with Mrs Apple in a Northampton-shire cottage. They quarrel, have adventures and entertain dangerous strangers. (*Original*)

LITTLE PETE STORIES *Leila Berg*
More favourites from *Listen With Mother*, about a small boy who plays mostly by himself. Illustrated by Peggy Fortnum.

THE HAPPY ORPHELINE *Natalie Savage Carlson*
A BROTHER FOR THE ORPHELINES
The 20 little orphaned girls who live with Madame Flattot are terrified of being adopted because they are so happy.

FIVE DOLLS IN A HOUSE *Helen Clare*
A little girl called Elizabeth finds a way of making herself small and
visits her dolls in their own house.

TELL ME A STORY *Eileen Colwell*
TELL ME ANOTHER STORY
TIME FOR A STORY
Stories, verses, and finger plays for children of 3 to 6, collected by the
greatest living expert on the art of children's story-telling.

BAD BOYS *Eileen Colwell*
Twelve splendid stories about naughty boys, by favourite authors like
Helen Cresswell, Charlotte Hough, Barbara Softly and Ursula Moray
Williams. (Original)

MY NAUGHTY LITTLE SISTER *Dorothy Edwards*
MY NAUGHTY LITTLE SISTER'S FRIENDS
WHEN MY NAUGHTY LITTLE SISTER WAS GOOD
MY NAUGHTY LITTLE SISTER AND BAD HARRY
These now famous stories were originally told by a mother to her own
children. Ideal for reading aloud. For ages 4 to 8.

MISS HAPPINESS AND MISS FLOWER *Rumer Godden*
Nona was lonely far away from her home in India, and the two dainty
Japanese dolls, Miss Happiness and Miss Flower, were lonely too.
But once Nona started building them a proper Japanese house they
all felt happier. Illustrated by Jean Primrose.

THE YOUNG PUFFIN BOOK OF VERSE *Barbara Ireson*
A deluge of poems about such fascinating subjects as birds and bal-
loons, mice and moonshine, farmers and frogs, pigeons and pirates,
especially chosen to please young people of four to eight. (*Original*)

SOMETHING TO MAKE *Felicia Law*
A varied and practical collection of things for children to make from
odds and ends around the house, with very little extra outlay, by an
experienced teacher of art and handicrafts. For children of 6 up.
(*Original*)

THIS LITTLE PUFFIN ... *Elizabeth Matterson*
A treasury of nursery games, finger plays and action songs, collected with the aid of nursery school teachers all over the British Isles. For parents of under-fives. (*Original*)

MEET MARY KATE *Helen Morgan*
Charmingly told stories of a four-year-old's everyday life in the country. Illustrated by Shirley Hughes.

PUFFIN BOOK OF NURSERY RHYMES
Peter and Iona Opie
The first comprehensive collection of nursery rhymes to be produced as a paperback, prepared for Puffins by the leading authorities on children's lore. 220 pages, exquisitely illustrated on every page by Pauline Baynes. (*Original*)

MRS PEPPERPOT TO THE RESCUE *Alf Prøysen*
MRS PEPPERPOT IN THE MAGIC WOOD
MRS PEPPERPOT'S OUTING
More stories about Mrs Pepperpot in which she goes to school in Rita's satchel, hides in a cat basket with the kittens, rides on a rocket, and plays matchbox cars with the baby mice in her cupboard.

THE SECRET SHOEMAKERS *James Reeves*
A dozen of Grimm's least-known fairy tales retold with all a poet's magic, and illustrated sympathetically by Edward Ardizzone.

ROM-BOM-BOM AND OTHER STORIES *Antonia Ridge*
A collection of animal stories written by the distinguished children's author and broadcaster. For 4 to 8 year olds.

DEAR TEDDY ROBINSON *Joan G. Robinson*
ABOUT TEDDY ROBINSON
TEDDY ROBINSON HIMSELF
KEEPING UP WITH TEDDY ROBINSON
Teddy Robinson was Deborah's teddy bear and such a very nice, friendly cuddly bear that he went everywhere with her and had even more adventures than she did.

THE ADVENTURES OF GALLDORA *Modwena Sedgwick*
NEW ADVENTURES OF GALLDORA

This lovable rag doll belonged to Marybell, who wasn't always very careful to look after her, so Galldora was always getting lost – in a field with a scarecrow, on top of a roof, and in all sorts of other strange places.

SOMETHING TO DO *Septima*

Suggestions for games to play and things to make and do each month, from January to December. It is designed to help mothers with young children at home. (*Original*)

PONDER AND WILLIAM *Barbara Softly*
PONDER AND WILLIAM ON HOLIDAY
PONDER AND WILLIAM AT HOME

Ponder the panda looks after William's pyjamas and is a wonderful companion in these all-the-year-round adventures. Illustrated by Diana John. (*Originals*)

CLEVER POLLY AND THE STUPID WOLF
POLLY AND THE WOLF AGAIN *Catherine Storr*

Clever Polly manages to think of lots of good ideas to stop the stupid wolf from eating her . . .

DANNY FOX *David Thomson*
DANNY MEETS A STRANGER
DANNY FOX AT THE PALACE

Clever Danny Fox helps the Princess to marry the fisherman she loves and comes safely home to his hungry family. (*Originals*)

GEORGE *Agnes Sligh Turnbull*

George was good at arithmetic, and housekeeping, and at keeping children happy and well behaved. The pity of it was that he was a rabbit so Mr Weaver didn't believe in him. Splendid for six-year-olds and over.

LITTLE O *Edith Unnerstad*

The enchanting story of the youngest of the Pip Larsson family.

THE URCHIN *Edith Unnerstad*

The Urchin is only five years old, but already he has the Larsson family at sixes and sevens with his ingenious tricks and adventures.

LITTLE RED FOX *Alison Uttley*

Little Red Fox was all alone in the great wood until kind Mr and Mrs Badger decided to adopt him and bring him up with their own two children.

MAGIC IN MY POCKET *Alison Uttley*

A selection of short stories by this well-loved author, especially good for five- and six-year-olds.

THE PENNY PONY *Barbara Willard*

Cathy and Roger found the pony in a junk shop. They wanted a live pony more than anything else in the world, but this one looked as if it might toss its head at any moment.

GOBBOLINO THE WITCH'S CAT *Ursula Moray Williams*

Gobbolino's mother was ashamed of him because his eyes were blue instead of green, and he wanted to be loved instead of learning spells. So he goes in search of a friendly kitchen. Illustrated by the author.

ADVENTURES OF THE LITTLE WOODEN HORSE
Ursula Moray Williams

To help his master, a brave little horse sets out to sell himself and brings home a great fortune.